Sarah May and the New Red Dress

Sarah May
and the
New Red Dress

written by Andrea Spalding
illustrated by Janet Wilson

ORCA BOOK PUBLISHERS

I wasn't always Grandma, you know, bespectacled and stiff-kneed.

     Once I was Sarah May.

     I wasn't always grey, you know, with wrinkled hands and feet and a surprised morning face at the old lady in the mirror.

     Once I was Sarah
          Sarah of the Sea Shore
             Sarah of the West Wind
                Yes, I was Sarah May.

Come, let me tell you about her.

"Sarah May needs a new dress," said Mother. "But it must be a dress that will last."

"It must be a dress that is cheap," said Father.

"Please let it be a red dress," I whispered to the West Wind.

The West Wind chuckled, danced the curtains and ruffled my hair.

We drove the pony trap to Mr. Corbett's general store. He sold fishnets and floats, hooks and bait, pans and dishes, hoes and rakes, pails and shovels, boots and shoes, sugar and salt, bacon and eggs, hammers, nails, needles, threads ... and dresses.

None of them was red.

"These are too expensive," said Father.

"Then I'll make a dress ..." said Mother.

"Red's a nice color," I suggested.

"... with some material that will last a long time without showing the dirt. Dark blue would be good."

Mr. Corbett measured three yards of dismal blue, wrapped it in brown paper, tied a loop in the string and gave it to me.

The wind shrugged and blew the sawdust in swirls across the floor.

I walked slowly along the wharf with the parcel in
my hand. "I hate dark blue," I muttered crossly to
the wind.

"Waaaiit and seeeee," the West Wind sang in my ears.

Mother measured and cut and pinned and sewed until the dress was finished. It fitted me with room to grow.

"You look very grown up," Father approved. "A dress like that will last a good long time."

"It's a very smart and sensible color," agreed Mother.

I sighed as the dress flapped around my calves. "I wish I liked it," I whispered to the wind.

"Yooouuu wiiiiilllll," the West Wind whispered back.

When I climbed the cliffs to watch the baby eagles taking their first flight, the dress tripped me. When Merrilegs and I galloped across the pasture, the dress flapped and scared her.

When I rowed out into the bay to fish, the dress caught on the side of the boat and bunched around the oars. "I really don't like this dress," I told the West Wind. "We have to do something about it."

The wind skittered away and set all the buttercups nodding.

On Sunday, my family climbed into the pony trap and we drove to church.

"Ah, Mr. and Mrs. Lydon," said the preacher. "Could you join us for lunch after the service?"

"Oh, dear," said Mother. "We should go home and feed the hens and collect the eggs."

"Sarah May is growing up," said Father. "Could you drive Merrilegs home on your own and see to the hens?" he asked.

"Of course," I answered. "I'll be as sensible as this dress."

I could hear the wind laughing in the bell tower.

Merrilegs and I set off. She danced her hooves along
the beach trail, copying the dancing waves. We
sauntered up to the point to enjoy the view, but as we
rounded the headland, there sat a big black cloud ... waiting.

"Watch this," chuckled the West Wind, and it began to blow.

The sunlight was suddenly shut off. Gusts of wind blew Merrilegs' mane and tail straight out, and I shivered as my hair and dress flapped and slapped me.

Down came the rain.

Pear-shaped drops plopped around us. They were hard and heavy, and soon Merrilegs and I were wet clear through. The rain dripped from my nose, dropped from my hem and puddled around my toes in a big, black puddle.

I stared. Black rain?

I held out my hand and clear rain splashed in the palm. I looked down at my feet again. A slow, dark drip dropped from the hem of my dress.

I reined in Merrilegs, jumped out of the trap and danced
across the headland.
    "Oh, thank you thank you, Wind,
Thank you thank you, Rain."
    I sang at the top of my voice, as I whirled and twirled
among the raindrops and watched the dark blue dye drip
from my sensible dress.

"Oh, Sarah May, you poor, poor thing," crooned Mother when I arrived home. "Soaked to the skin, and your new dress ruined."

The next day Mother bleached the ruined dress. "Ride to the store and choose a packet of dye," she told me. "Get a good strong color that will cover the streaky parts."

Guess what color I bought?

We soaked the dress in the dye for a good long time.
Mother stirred it around with a long, wooden spoon.
Then she rinsed it in a bowl of vinegar.
"To set the color forever," she explained.

"I told you to wait and see," laughed the West Wind as
it swirled my dress and spattered the drips around the yard.

In my new red dress I could almost float to the top of the cliffs to watch the soaring eagles. Mother liked my red dress. She could see me fishing even when I was out in the middle of the bay.

Merrilegs loved my dress. We galloped together across the headland, and it streamed behind us like a crusader's flag.

Father laughed. "I'm glad that sensible dress didn't make you grow up too fast."

I wasn't always Grandma, you know, bespectacled and grey.

I was Sarah of the Sea Shore
Sarah of the West Wind
Sarah of the Red Dress

Yes, I'm still Sarah May.